P9-CAA-995

THANK YOU NOTES

THANK YOU NOTES

JIMMY FALLON
with **THE WRITERS OF LATE NIGHT**

GRAND CENTRAL
PUBLISHING
NEW YORK BOSTON

Grand Central Publishing
Hachette Book Group
237 Park Avenue
New York, NY 10017

www.HachetteBookGroup.com
Printed in the United States of America

First Edition: May 2011

10 9 8 7 6 5 4 3 2 1

Cover design by Nick Caruso.
Interior design by Renato Stanisic.

Grand Central Publishing is a division of Hachette Book Group, Inc.
The Grand Central Publishing name and logo is a trademark of Hachette Book Group, Inc.

The publisher is not responsible for websites (or their content) that are not owned by the publisher.

Library of Congress Control Number: 2011920745

ISBN: 978-0-89296-741-4

This book is dedicated to the writers of Late Night with Jimmy Fallon.

It would not have been possible without you. Well, without you and my flawless delivery.

Acknowledgments

....

I may "write" the thank you notes, but thank you to the people who actually wrote them:

David Angelo

Alex Baze

Michael Blieden

Patrick Borelli

Gerard Bradford

Jeremy Bronson

Mike DiCenzo

Janine DiTullio

Ben Dougan

Wayne Federman

Anthony Jeselnik

Casey Jost

Eric Ledgin

Tim McAuliffe

A.D. Miles

Morgan Murphy

Amy Ozols

Bobby Patton

Gavin Purcell

Diallo Riddle

Jon Rineman

Bashir Salahuddin

Justin Shanes

Michael Shoemaker

Bobby Tisdale

Ali Waller

This book could not have been put together without the hard work of Kelly Powers, John MacDonald, Joel Knutson, Beth Rodgers, Edmond Hawkins, Lloyd Bishop, Brian McDonald, Risa Abrams, Erica Lancaster, Caroline Eppright, and Nick Caruso.

Thank you to the *Late Night* team for getting me through every day: Michael Shoemaker, Gavin Purcell, A.D. Miles, Hillary Hunn, Alice Michaels, and Katie Hockmeyer.

Thanks to Eric Kranzler, Simon Green, Jeff Jacobs, Peter Levine, Tom Rowan, and Ben Greenberg.

Thanks to everyone at NBC, especially Rick Ludwin, Nick Bernstein, Rebecca Marks, Marc Graboff, Amber James, Nate Kirtman, Kim Niemi, Drew Rowley, Steve Coulter, Ed Prince, Leslie Schwartz, Joni Camacho, Neysa Siefert, Scott Radloff, and Jessica Nubel.

Thanks to The Roots for everything and to James Poyser for his inspirational accompaniment.

Thank you to my wife Nancy and my parents, Jim and Gloria Fallon.

And finally, thank you "thank you list at the beginning of this book" for being longer than the actual book. What the hell is that about?

Introduction: A Thank You to the Reader

....

Thank you, reader, for buying this book. Because of you, I just made enough money to buy part of one beer. So in a way you, and a bunch of other readers, just bought me a beer. And when I drink that beer, I will stare into the glass and say a quiet "thank you." Everyone else in the bar will wonder why I'm talking to my drink, but so what? This is between you and me.

Me thanking you for buying this book. Unless you got it as a gift. In which case, you should go find that person and thank him or her.

Now that everybody's good and thanked, go ahead and enjoy the book. I promise you'll laugh. If you don't, then come find me at the bar. I'll buy you part of one beer.

Thank you

...the word *moist*, for being the worst word ever. I think I speak for all Americans when I say that we don't want you as a word anymore. God, I hate you.

pl **mohels** *also* ...
-(h)e-'lĕm\ : a person w

one of two equal or a

... : to work hard : DRUDGE — **moil** *n*

moil·er *n*

moi·ré \mò-'rā, mwä-\ *or* **moire** *same or* 'mȯir, 'mwär\
: a fabric (as silk) having a watered appearance
moist \'mȯist\ *adj* : slightly or moderately wet — **moist**
adv — **moist·ness** *n*
moist·en \'mȯi-s²n\ *vb* : to make or become moist

... **mod·eled** *or* m...
... FASHION
... 1 : serving as o...
... 2 : being a...
... ⟨a ~ airplane⟩
... \'mȯ-dəm, -,dem\ *n* ...
... one device (as a c...
... another (as a teleph...
... \'ma-də-rət\ *adj*
... 2 : AVERAGE;
... or effect. 4 : not e...
... *adv* — **mod·er·...ness** *n*
... \'ma-də-,rāt\ *vb* -at·ed; -at·ing 1 : to lessen
... : TEMPER 2 : to act as a moderator —
... \,ma-də-'rā-shən\ *n*

Thank you

...Taco Bell Chihuahua, for your many years of faithful service as a mildly offensive Mexican stereotype.

Thank you

...tequila. You know why. . . Oh, all right, I'll just say it. Thank you for making me puke up everything I ate the night before. I lost two pounds!

the **Real Housewives**
OF ATLANTA

JIMMY FALLON

Thank you

...*Real Housewives of Atlanta*, for demonstrating a universal truth: Idiots like me will always watch idiots like you fight on TV. You will forever be in my TiVo.

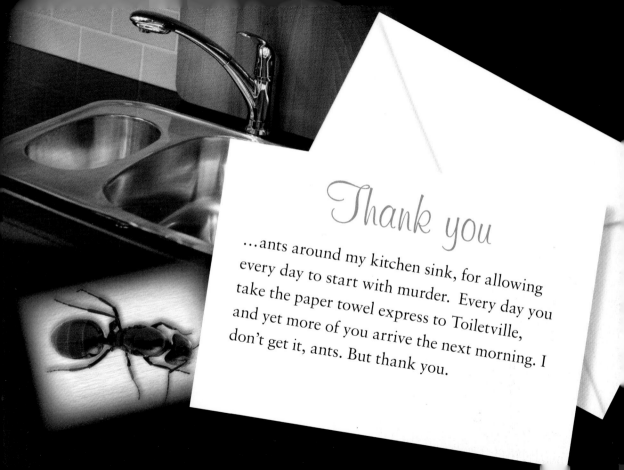

Thank you

...ants around my kitchen sink, for allowing every day to start with murder. Every day you take the paper towel express to Toiletville, and yet more of you arrive the next morning. I don't get it, ants. But thank you.

Thank you

…DVR remote control, for your incredibly confusing response time. I push rewind five times and nothing happens, so I push it again and suddenly I'm all the way back to the beginning of the show, so I have to fast-forward again. Why won't you just work, DVR remote? You're so confusing. Thank you.

JIMMY FALLON

Snuggie
For Dogs

Extra Small

See back panel for sizing guide

The Blanket Coat With Sleeves!

Thank you

...Dog Snuggie®, for allowing us to embarrass animals in a way I never imagined possible. You did it. Thanks for that.

Thank you

…slow-walking family walking in front of me on the sidewalk. No, please, take your time. And definitely spread out, too, so you create a barricade of idiots. I am so thankful that you forced me to walk into the street and risk getting hit by a car in order to pass you so I could resume walking at a normal human pace.

Thank you

...preseason football, for having all the excitement, commercials, and time-outs of the regular season, but with none of the mattering. I appreciate it. Thank you.

Thank you

...guy with the $10,000 sound system in his $800 car, for driving down Broadway this afternoon. You're loud. You're proud. You're in a '91 Tercel. Thank you.

Thank you

…guy at my dry cleaners, for charging me $11 to clean a dress shirt. It clearly doesn't cost that much, but you know I'll pay it anyway because I'm not really sure what you do and how much it should cost. In fact, I'm 99 percent sure that all you did was iron it and put a plastic sheet over it.

Thank you

...fantasy football draft, for letting me know that even in my fantasies, I am bad at sports.

PENILE
CANCER

…newly discovered virus linked to penile cancer, for making me say the words *penile cancer*. I don't think I have penile cancer, but maybe I'm just in penile. You know, penile is not just a river in Egypt. Sorry. . . I mean thanks. I should probably get it checked out.

Thank you

...Apple, for adding a camera to the iPod Nano. Now it's just like the iPhone except it can't make calls. So basically, it's just like the iPhone.

Thank you

...guy in the revolving door who isn't pulling his weight, for letting me handle all the pushing responsibilities while you handle all the waiting responsibilities. No, let me get it for you. You're the king of the hotel entrance.

Thank you

2 button on my keyboard. What is it

gain? Oh, that's right—nothing.

Thank you

...Dad, for discovering text messaging. I really liked that text you sent with the smiley face, but not as much as the 27 blank text messages you sent right after. They kept me awake. Thanks, Dad.

Thank you

...shampoo ... or as I like to call you when I run out of soap, "soap."

NEW

SOAP

2 in 1

dandruff formula

13.3 FL OZ (400 mL)

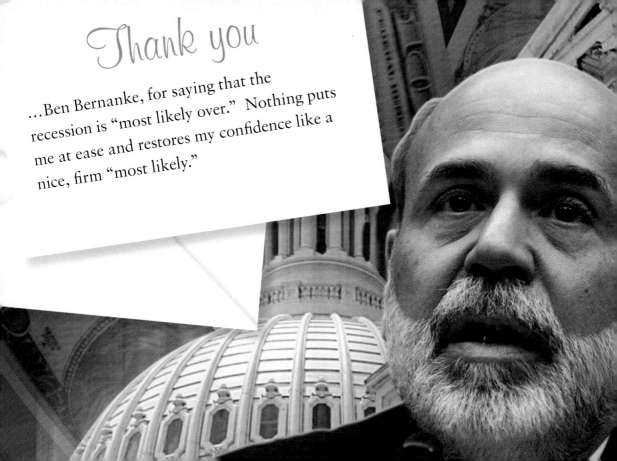

Thank you

...Ben Bernanke, for saying that the recession is "most likely over." Nothing puts me at ease and restores my confidence like a nice, firm "most likely."

Thank you

…"People You May Know" feature on Facebook, for never introducing me to a single person that I actually want to know, ever. More accurately, your title should be "People I Do Know but Am Avoiding." Thanks.

Thank you

...pop-up ads where it's impossible to find where to click CLOSE. Or the ones that suddenly appear and block you from clicking on a link you really want to click, and then disappear as soon as you move your cursor away, only to reappear when you try again. You are so awesoooome!

Thank you

...hotel minibar, for charging $7 for a mini Toblerone. And thank you, Me, for eating three of them.

Thank you

...2000 Flushes toilet cleaner, for not lying and saying that you last for 3,000 flushes. Because, the truth is ... you could. I mean, it's not like I'm going to count flushes or anything. OR WILL I???

Thank you

...guy on the street who let one go while listening to his iPod. Just because you can't hear it, doesn't mean it didn't happen. It happened.

Thank you

...guy who uses the urinal right next to me even though there are literally ten open urinals. Why not put your arm around my shoulder while we're at it? Maybe we can reach over and flush each other's toilets. You know, just a couple of "synchronized pee pals." Thanks.

Thank you

...the Fall, for arriving this week. I was really getting tired of Summer's bullshit.

Thank you

...vegan food, for being a healthy alternative to high-fat, meat-based diets. And for tasting like microwaved paper towels.

elders of a district

pre·school \\'prē-ˌskül\\ *adj* : of or relating to the period in a child's life from infancy to the age of five or six — **pre-**
school·er \\-ˌskü-lər\\ *n*
preschool *n* : NURSERY SCHOOL
pre·science \\'pre-shəns, 'prē-\\ *n* : foreknowledge of events; *also* : FORESIGHT — **pre·scient** \\-shənt, -shē-ənt\\
pre·scribe \\pri-'skrīb\\ *vb* **pre·scribed; pre·scrib·ing** 1
: to lay down as a guide or rule of action 2 : to direct the use of (as a

...listing of the ministers

nist country
¹**pre·soak**
²**pre·soak**
preparation
pre·sort
before deliv
¹**press** \\'pres\\
machine for
: PRESSURE
ly pressed
the process
tablishment

Thank you

...the word *prescient*. I'm not exactly sure what
you mean, but I try to slip you into conversation
when I don't think the person I'm talking to
knows what you mean, either. I knew they
didn't know what I was talking about—it was
the perfect example of being prescient. By the
way, I got you a birthday prescient.

Thank you

...leaves, for starting to change color. You can disguise yourselves however you like . . . but I still know it's you.

Thank you

…guy in his fifties who jogs in spandex Lycra pants. The good news is, regular exercise at your age can greatly reduce your chances of heart attack, disease, and stroke. The bad news is, I can see your nuts.

Thank you

…Chinese delivery place, for giving me three sets of utensils when—SURPRISE!—it was just me eating. Are you trying to tell me that one person shouldn't eat all this food? Next time why not take it further? Why not have the fortune cookie tell me to "take human bites." Or say "Are you done now, fat ass?"

Thank you

...haters, for giving rappers so much to talk about.

Thank you

...NASA, for firing that missile at the moon. I think that sent a clear message to other lifeless rocks in the solar system that their constant orbiting will no longer be tolerated.

Thank you

...electrical outlets in Australia, for making me feel like I'm plugging my hair dryer into the mask from *Scream*.

Thank you

...people who count their money at the ATM and then file it away slowly while I stand behind them, for not feeling burdened by my presence. I'm just going to stand here silently getting madder and madder, and when you turn around and apologize to me, I'm going to say "no problem" in the most upbeat voice you've ever heard.

Thank you

...gym, for being exactly like my grandpa—always there for me, even though I only visit you twice a year.

Thank you

...customer service guy in India who calls himself "Todd," thinking that will trick me into thinking he's actually in Omaha and not New Delhi. Nice try, "Todd." Hee hee ... Yes, I'll hold.

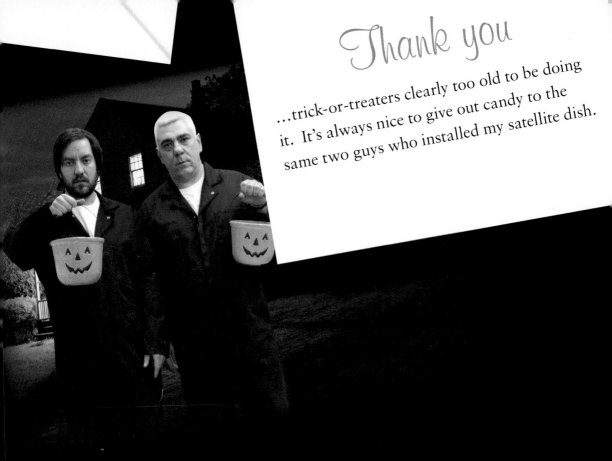

Thank you

...trick-or-treaters clearly too old to be doing it. It's always nice to give out candy to the same two guys who installed my satellite dish.

Thank you

...raisins, for decades of faithful service as the Halloween treat of choice for hippies, cheapskates, and assholes.

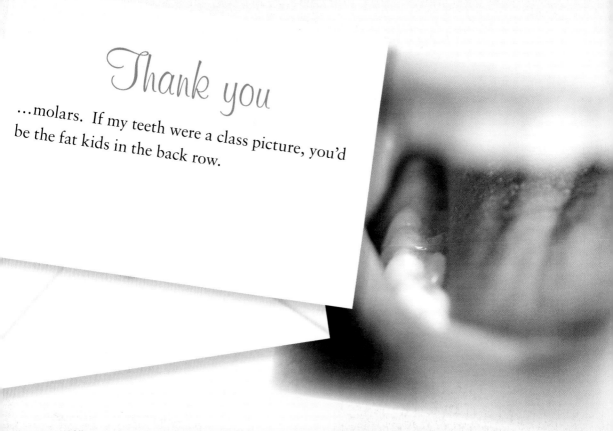

Thank you

...molars. If my teeth were a class picture, you'd be the fat kids in the back row.

HELLO
my name is

Lloyd

Thank you

...the name Lloyd, for starting with two Ls.
I'm glad both those *L*s were there, because
otherwise I would have called you "Loyd."

Thank you

...Christmas decorations, for going up right after Halloween. Nothing says "holidays" like seeing my neighbor replace his plastic Dracula with a plastic baby Jesus.

Thank you

...flour, for keeping the paper sack container business alive. Don't want to change your packaging, huh? Whenever I buy you I feel like I'm Charles Ingalls buying something from Oleson's store on credit.

Thank you

…dishwasher, for never getting cocky about how clean your dishes are. Because we both know that I wash them too much before I put them in you. Yup, you have a pretty sweet deal, don't you, dishwasher? Dishwasher, I'm just fooling around, why do you look so freaked out? Hold on a second, dishwasher, wait a minute, are you wearing a wire?! What the … Hey, this dishwasher's a cop! You betrayed me!

Thank you

...PEZ dispensers, for being little creatures that vomit candy out of their necks. You're awesome.

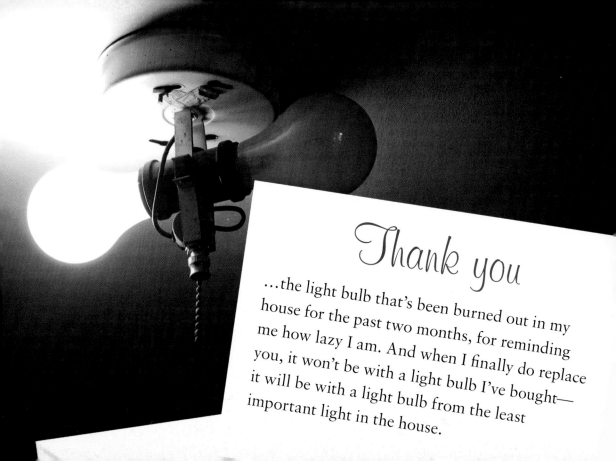

Thank you

...the light bulb that's been burned out in my house for the past two months, for reminding me how lazy I am. And when I finally do replace you, it won't be with a light bulb I've bought— it will be with a light bulb from the least important light in the house.

Thank you

...zebras, for showing me what horses would look like if I were on acid.

Thank you

…person unwrapping a cough drop in the movie theater. I know you think that by unwrapping your lozenge very slowly it's somehow less offensive. It's not. I can hear every damn crinkle of that wrapper. Wait, are you rewrapping it just so you can unwrap it again? Thank you.

Thank you

...Febreze, for allowing dirt and filth to live freely among us in total secrecy.

Thank you

...Chili's menus, for listing how many calories are in your food. I'M IN A CHILI'S! What part of "I don't give a crap" do you not understand?

Thank you

...cockroaches living under the sink in my bathroom. First there were two of you, then there were four, then ten, then thirty. I don't know how you reproduce so quickly, but I can only come to one conclusion: You guys are sluts.

Thank you

...microbreweries, for making my alcoholism seem like a neat hobby.

Thank you

...nickels, for being the redheaded stepchild of the coin community. You're so thick, yet you're worth so little. You're like the quarter's fatter, less successful brother.

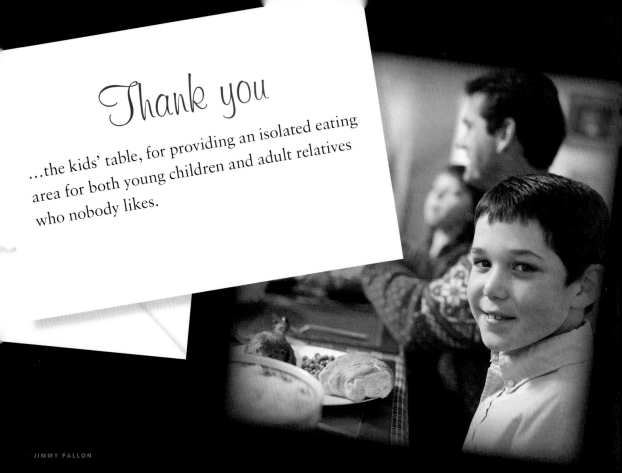

Thank you

...the kids' table, for providing an isolated eating area for both young children and adult relatives who nobody likes.

Thank you

...stuffing, for always being delicious, even though you're cooked inside a turkey's butt.

Thank you

...the choice between the sofa bed and the air mattress at my parents' house, for making me choose whether I want to sleep on a series of poorly placed metal bars or on an inflatable raft filled with cold air that leaks until I'm sleeping on the floor.

Thank you

...post-Thanksgiving-dinner relaxation rituals, for being the one time when Uncle Gary can unbuckle his pants in front of the whole family and not get sent to jail.

Thank you

...gizzard bag inside the turkey. If I was interested in coming face-to-face with a moist bag of vital organs, I'd take a look at the old people across the table.

Thank you

...Christmas tree farms. You're pretty much the only places in the world where a man carrying an axe in one arm and a toddler in the other can be considered normal.

Thank you

...wishbones, for being the final "fuck you" to the turkey I have just devoured.

Thank you

...office Christmas parties. In these times of economic stress and uncertainty, it's important that employees can come together in a relaxed atmosphere and find out who's the biggest slut in Accounting. (It's Jessica.)

Thank you

...guy whose chair made a farting noise, for spending the next 20 minutes awkwardly shifting around trying to re-create the noise so people would know it was just the chair.

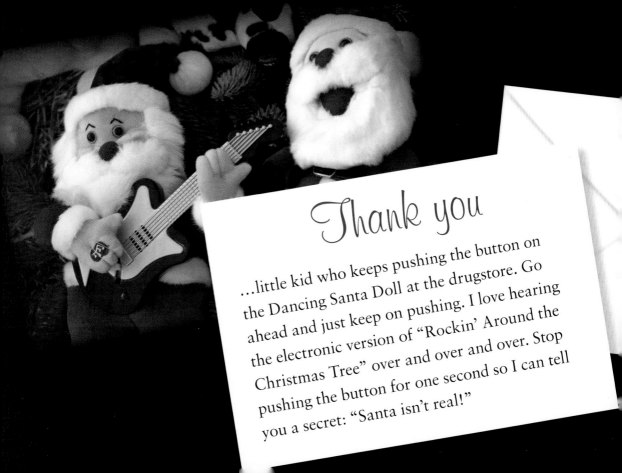

Thank you

...little kid who keeps pushing the button on the Dancing Santa Doll at the drugstore. Go ahead and just keep on pushing. I love hearing the electronic version of "Rockin' Around the Christmas Tree" over and over and over. Stop pushing the button for one second so I can tell you a secret: "Santa isn't real!"

Thank you

...to the radiator next to my bed. The noises you make resound in my head. The gurgling, the knocking, the hissing, the clanging. The whistling, chortling, ringing, and banging—they wake me and plague me, such is the norm. But this ancient device keeps me toasty and warm.

Thank you

...guy who buys an entire outfit from one store. You clearly saw the mannequin and thought, *That's the one.*

Thank you

…Christmas family newsletters that fill my day with useful information like "Great News: Carolyn got her braces off!" and "Great News: Aaron made the basketball team." Here's some news: "Nobody gives a shit!"

Happy Holidays!

Christmas is a time for reflection, so what better time to look back on 2009? It was quite the year for the Thompson clan!!!

Great News! Carolyn got her braces off! As you all know, she's had them since the fifth grade, and her orthodontist said that she was an "A+ brusher." She was also an "A+ student," as she made the seventh grade Honor Roll in the second semester!

And while we're in the Great News department for the Thompson kids, let's not forget that Aaron made the Freshman JV Basketball team! Over 30 kids tried out, and Aaron was one of only 22 that made the team. Now all he has to do is grow a few more inches! (Hopefully he takes after Uncle David!!!).

As for me and Mark, things have been going good! Perhaps the biggest move is that this winter, we welcomed a new member of the family! (No, not another kid, ha ha!) It's our beloved puppy Buster (or more formally, Buster Rex Thompson the 3rd)! Hope everyone is well, and has a happy and healthy holiday season!!!

Cindy, Mark,
Carolyn, Aaron,
& Buster!

Thank you

...pizza box, for being impossible to dispose of. Thank you for not fitting inside any trash bag or trash can or trash chute ever built by humans, and thank you for popping open and spilling half-eaten crust on me whenever I try to throw you away.

Thank you

...people who give me homemade jam as a gift. What are we, Quakers? Exactly how much jam do you think I use? You know this is going to sit in my fridge for three years until I throw it out to make room for beer, right? Just checking.

☐ I agree to the terms and conditions

INSTALL

Thank you

..."Yes, I Agree to the Terms and Conditions"
box I have to click in order to install software.
You know full well I didn't actually read the
terms and conditions. For all I know, I just
agreed to become the new face of herpes. But
I'm still gonna click you.

Thank you

...first week in January, for being the one week of the year when there are people at my gym who are fatter than I am.

Thank you

…New Year's resolutions, for being like Las Vegas wedding vows: half-assed promises made by drunken idiots.

Thank you

...adult mittens, for allowing me to give people the finger without them knowing it.

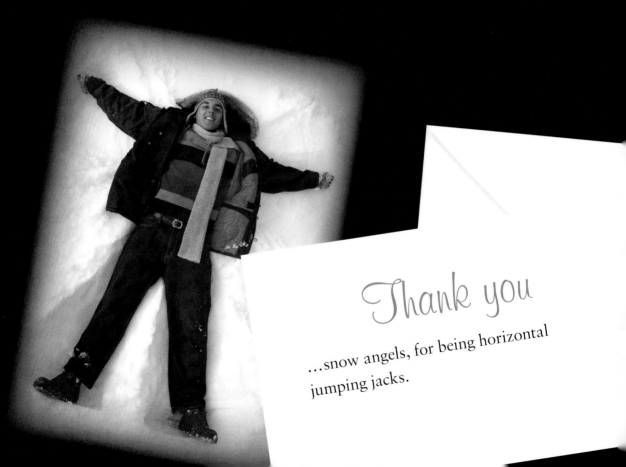

Thank you

...snow angels, for being horizontal jumping jacks.

Thank you

...my checked luggage. I hear you enjoyed Puerto Rico this Christmas vacation.

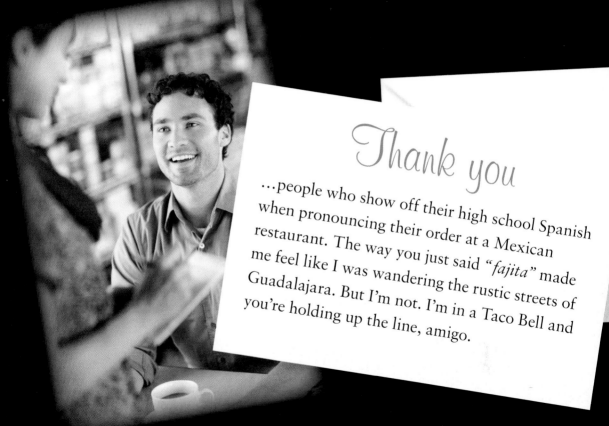

Thank you

…people who show off their high school Spanish when pronouncing their order at a Mexican restaurant. The way you just said *"fajita"* made me feel like I was wandering the rustic streets of Guadalajara. But I'm not. I'm in a Taco Bell and you're holding up the line, amigo.

Thank you

...tai chi, for being the perfect way to defend myself against an army of invisible slow-motion ninjas.

Thank you

…sliders, for tricking me into thinking you're a perfectly appropriate appetizer. Would I like to start my meal with a regular-size hamburger? Of course not! But I WILL have six TINY hamburgers because that's totally different. Thank you.

Thank you

...ponytails, for turning the backs of girls' heads into horses' butts.

Thank you

...horseradish, for being neither a radish nor of a horse. What you are is a liar food. (I'm looking at you, too, Grape Nuts.)

Thank you

…pen I just put in my mouth and started chewing on, for already having bite marks on you to remind me that, Oh yeah, you're not my pen.

Thank you

...box of Valentine's chocolates, for being like candy land mines. I was hoping for macadamia nut, but I guess I'll have to settle for this thing that tastes like soup and oranges.

Thank you

...lasers, for being spelled with an *s* even though you'd be totally more badass if you were spelled with a *z*. Just sayin'.

Thank you

...people with sesquipedalophobia, which is the fear of long words. You picked the wrong thing to call your fear.

sesquipedalophobia

Thank you

…typewriters. What the hell, man?! You guys were cocky as hell all the way up to the '80s. "Can't do business without me! Good luck writing a novel without me around!" Now look at you . . . Bunch of obsolete sons of bitches sitting around like old metal turds. *Click clack! Click clack!* Yeah, right.

Thank you

...certain days when I can see the sun and the moon in the sky at the same time. You make me feel like I'm Luke Skywalker on his home planet of Tatooine, concerned about his aunt and uncle and restless for adventure.

Thank you

...sweater vests. You're a great way to keep warm while telling your arms to go screw themselves.

Thank you

...fake drawer in my kitchen. Even though I've lived with you for ten years, you still manage to fake me out. Come on, fake drawer!

Thank you

...hangers, for being like floating plastic shoulders.

Thank you

...New York, for being the only city in America with enough tall buildings for Spider-Man to do his thing. Could you imagine if Peter Parker was born in Santa Fe, New Mexico? LAAAME!

Thank you

…person I'm walking behind who happens to be going in the exact same direction, for making me feel like I'm following you. And thank you, my decision to joke "I'm not following you," for somehow not putting that person at ease.

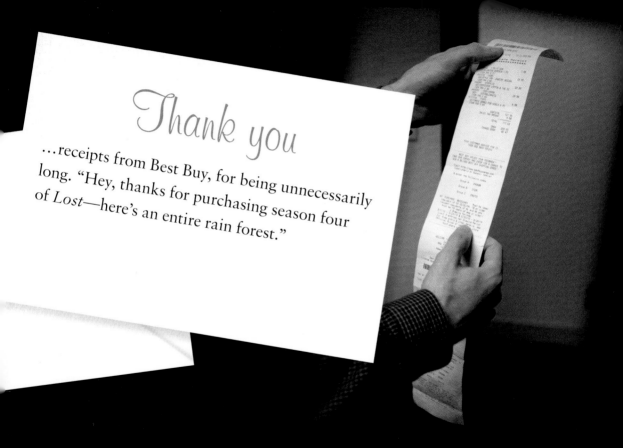

Thank you

…receipts from Best Buy, for being unnecessarily long. "Hey, thanks for purchasing season four of *Lost*—here's an entire rain forest."

Thank you

...ESPN Classic, for being a really exciting channel to watch if you just came out of a coma.

Thank you

...the expression "with all due respect," for letting me know when people are about to say something with zero respect.

"with all due respect..."

Thank you

...urinals that inexplicably have ice in them. You know exactly what I'm looking for—a nice pee on the rocks. Next time, can I get a twist of lime in there, too? Maybe a salted rim? Thanks.

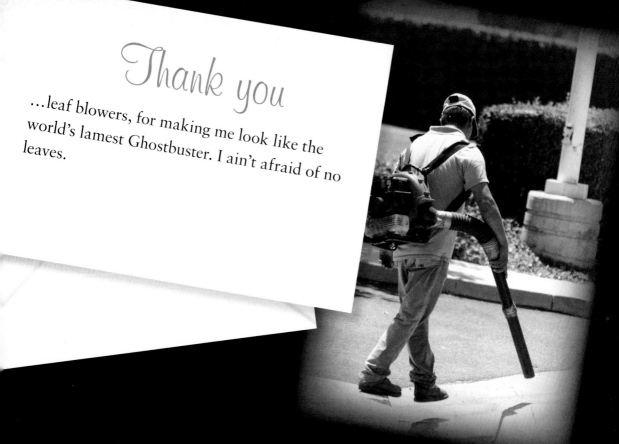

Thank you

...leaf blowers, for making me look like the world's lamest Ghostbuster. I ain't afraid of no leaves.

Thank you

...glass of water on my table last night at P. F. Chang's, for rippling when an overweight man walked by. I know you weren't TRYING to compare him to a dinosaur, but you just couldn't help yourself, could you?

Thank you

...people who insist on showing off ultrasound pictures of your unborn children. Just so you know, all those pictures look exactly the same: like charcoal drawings of an alien. For all you know, doctors just give the exact same picture to everyone and say, "There it is! There's your fetus!" And no one can ever tell the difference.

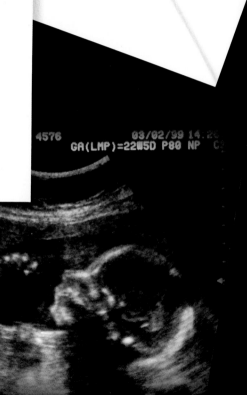

Thank you

...friend who loans me his jacket but doesn't tell me the pockets are full of used tissues. Snot cool, buddy. Snot cool.

Thank you

...bathroom attendant who hands me a towel, for making me feel guilty that I don't have a dollar to give you. And thank you, Me, for lying and saying that I'll bring an extra dollar the next time. We both know I'm never coming back to this bathroom.

Thank you

...Me from three months ago, who promised to get in shape during the winter. You lying sack of shit. It's 4:00 p.m.—put down the Cinnabon. (Next winter I swear I will.)

Thank you

…restaurants that advertise breakfast all day, for basically saying, "Try getting THIS at a place that isn't terrible."

BREAKFAST ALL DAY

Thank you

...people who say, "Wow, you're really photogenic," for not saying what you really mean: "Wow, you're really ugly in person."

Thank you

...softball, for being like baseball for women and drunks.

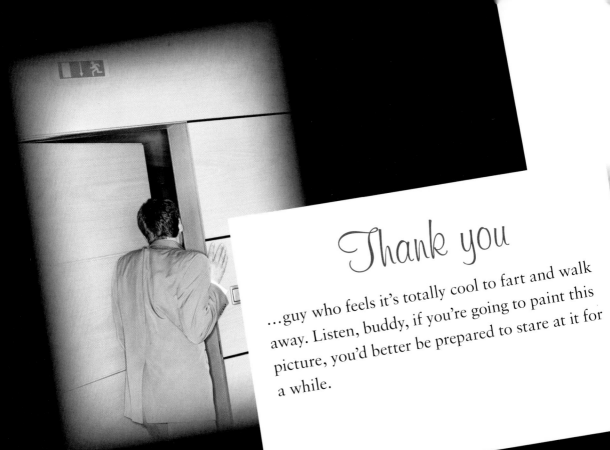

Thank you

...guy who feels it's totally cool to fart and walk away. Listen, buddy, if you're going to paint this picture, you'd better be prepared to stare at it for a while.

Thank you

...weather and traffic, for being the two things I can always talk about with old people.

Thank you

…pens at the ATM, for being attached to the deposit slip table by tiny chains. Don't flatter yourselves—no one's gonna steal you, you filthy germ sticks.

Thank you

...people who make me take my shoes off when I visit your house. I hope you enjoy your really, really, clean house where everybody feels uncomfortable and everything smells like feet.

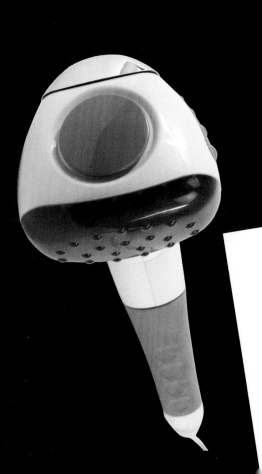

Thank you

...Brookstone, for always coming up with new and innovative ways to make vibrators for people too embarrassed to buy them at sex stores.

Thank you

...Mother's Day, for being exactly like Father's Day, except with people actually giving a crap.

happy mother's day

Thank you

...cotton candy, for making my grandmother's hair look delicious.

Thank you

...socks with sandals, for being a look that proudly declares to the world, "The people I'm friends with now are the only people I ever want to be friends with."

Thank you

…socks with sandals, for being a look that proudly declares to the world, "I've officially stopped trying."

Thank you

…socks with sandals, for being a look that proudly declares to the world, "I left my fanny pack at home."

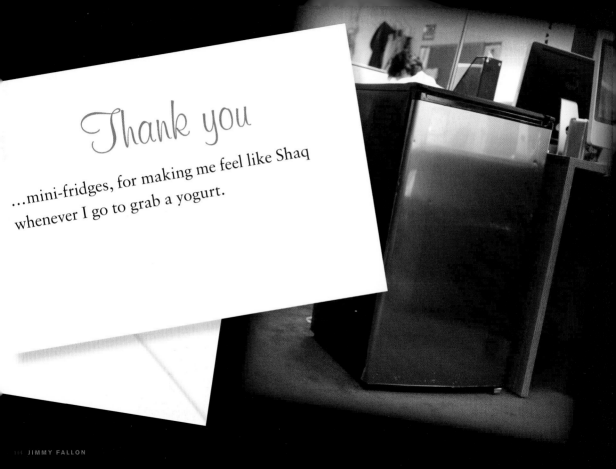

Thank you

...mini-fridges, for making me feel like Shaq whenever I go to grab a yogurt.

Thank you

…roosters, for being nature's way of saying, "Wake up, you lazy a-holes."

Thank you

...beach season, for helping us identify the people in our community who are completely incapable of shame.

Thank you

...toys that are impossible to remove from their packaging because they're secured with 36 twisty ties. It shouldn't be easier to steal a car than it is to remove a toy truck from its packaging.

Thank you

…teddy bears, for being way less judgmental than real bears when I try to spoon with you.

Thank you

…millipedes, for being approximately ten times more awesome than centipedes.

Thank you

...man in Washington who accidentally shot himself in the testicles at the hardware store. "Welcome to Ace Hardware—the bolts are in Aisle 5, the nuts are splattered all over Aisle 7."

Thank you

...graduations, for being a time when we come together and celebrate a bunch of kids who spent four long years getting at least a C−.

Thank you

…summer barbecues, for always featuring fun family games like horseshoes, croquet, and "Let's see how many daiquiris Grandma can drink before she gets racist."

Thank you

...fancy restaurant wine list, for providing me with plenty of notable choices to ignore while I look for the second-least-expensive bottle on the menu.

Thank you

...driver's license photo, for reminding me that there was at least one moment in my life when I looked exactly like a homeless serial killer.

Thank you

...gym that I go to. On the plus side, your treadmills have TVs on them. On the downside, your TVs have treadmills on them.

Thank you

...the YMCA, for officially changing your name to "the Y." I can't wait to hear the new hit song about you by the Village Person.

the **Y**

YMCA

NOTICE

WE DON'T SWIM IN YOUR TOILET

DON'T PEE IN OUR POOL

Thank you

...neighbors with swimming pools who put up signs that say, "We don't swim in your toilet, don't pee in our pool!" Pretty clever. But that's not going to stop me.

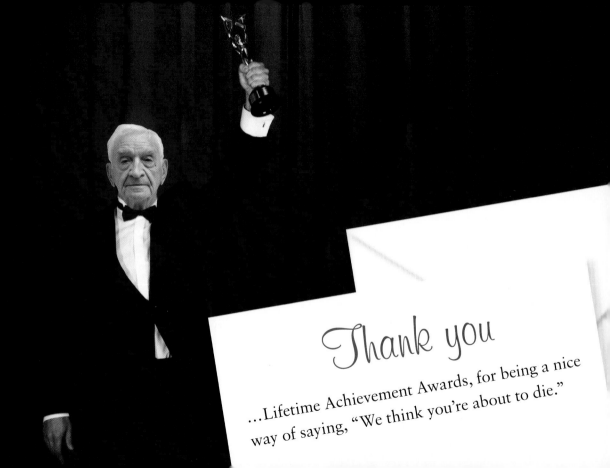

Thank you

...Lifetime Achievement Awards, for being a nice way of saying, "We think you're about to die."

Thank you

...2:30 in the morning, for always being the first sign that tomorrow's gonna suck.

Thank you

...guy at a urinal who reaches over to shake my hand with one hand while continuing your business with the other. Life is short, buddy, but it ain't that short.

OUTSTANDING DEBT

Thank you

...the term *outstanding debt*, for making it sound like it's awesome to owe people money.

Thank you

...hand sanitizer pumps in public restrooms, for supplying me with 90 percent of the germs I'm trying to kill.

Thank you

...alligators, for not being crocodiles—but also for being crocodiles as far as I'm concerned.

THESAURUS

Thank you

...thesaurus, for bettering my vocabulary. No, "enhancing" my vocabulary. Nay, "aggrandizing" my vocabulary. Yes, "aggrandizing"—that's the one.

Thank you

...friend getting married four thousand miles away, for making me feel bad that I'm not spending three thousand dollars to attend your wedding. I'll make you a deal: I'll go, but if you ever get divorced, you have to pay me three thousand dollars.

Thank you

...oscillating fans, for being soooo good, then not so good, then soooo good, then not so good, then soooo good.

Thank you

...smoothies, for being fat people's way of saying, "I'm drinking a milkshake, but I don't want to call it that."

Thank you

...Cool Ranch Doritos, for being so delicious that I almost forget you make my breath smell like dragon barf for seven hours after I eat you.

Thank you

...knife and fork, for keeping spoon in check. He made a move on my pasta last night, but you guys were there to show him what's what.

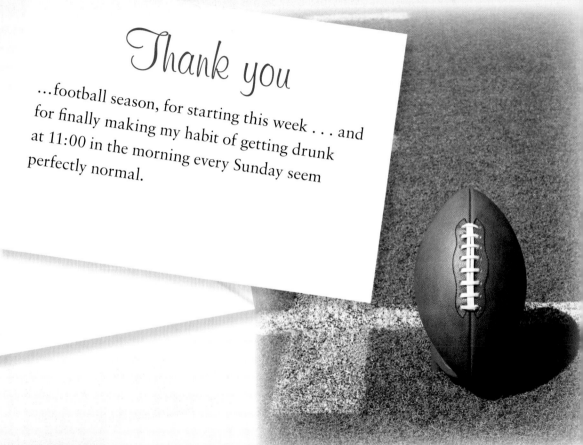

Thank you

...football season, for starting this week ... and for finally making my habit of getting drunk at 11:00 in the morning every Sunday seem perfectly normal.

Thank you

...paper clips, for being like staples for people who can't commit.

Thank you

...home gym, for being a monument to that one time when I wanted to get in shape.

Thank you

...the feeling that I lost my cell phone, even though I just put it in the wrong pocket. Those ten seconds of absolute terror did a great job of reminding me what a weak man I am.

Thank you

...fish cakes, for not even *trying* to sound good.

Thank you

...zip line, for being the fastest and most convenient way to travel between two trees.

Thank you

...enchilada, for looking like a burrito that just threw up all over itself.

Thank you

...new leather jacket, for being much heavier than I thought. Every time I put you on I feel like I'm getting X-rays at the dentist.

Thank you

...decaf coffee, for giving me the same stained teeth and stink-breath as regular coffee, with none of the pesky wakefulness and mental clarity.

Thank you

...wine cork collection. I know I never got around to making that corkboard—but look how much I drink!

Thank you

...fun-size candy, for calling yourself "fun" to distract me from the fact that you're smaller than regular candy. Nice try. They should call you "disappointment-size candy."

Peanut Butter

NET WT .55 OZ (15 g)

CRISPY

CANDY

Thank you

...hotel beds, for being so much more comfortable than regular beds . . . even though 24 hours ago, someone probably did something really disgusting on you.

Thank you

...tuna casserole, for being the sweatpants of food.

Thank you

...first sheet of a new toilet paper roll that won't tear off evenly so I have to scratch and claw and shred three layers of the roll just to get the thing started. But that's cool. I think I'll have the last laugh, since I know where you're ending up.

Thank you

...symbolism, for being, I don't know, sort of like a rose.

Thank you

…waterbeds, for answering the age-old question, "What would it be like to fall asleep on a giant breast implant?"

Thank you

...new pair of corduroys, for making that cool "whooshing" sound when I walk. Nothing signals the start of fall like the sound of people's fat thighs rubbing together.

Thank you

…onion rings, for being my favorite food, until I bite into you and I'm left with a cold, wet onion in my mouth and a tiny deep-fried steering wheel cover in my hand.

Thank you

...plastic cutlery, for reminding us all how strong bread can be.

Thank you

...women who put on their makeup in front of strangers while commuting to work. It's like you're creating a before-and-after photo right before our eyes.

Thank you

...older woman next to me in my yoga class, for ripping not one but two big ones during downward-facing dog. It's like that old saying, "One yoga toot, shame on you. Two yoga toots, you should probably go to the ladies' room."

Thank you

...chocolate chips, for not being called "sugar turds."

Thank you

…coarse wool sweaters, for having a relationship with my nipples that could best be described as "problematic."

Thank you

...gummy worms, for being excellent bait if I want to catch a Swedish Fish.

Thank you

...shorts weather, for reminding me that it's almost time to go apeshit on my milky-white chicken legs with a tube of tinted bronzer.

Photography Credits

....